MW01056593

DISCARD

SOMETHING HAPPENED IN OUR PARK

STANDING TOGETHER AFTER GUN VIOLENCE

BY ANN HAZZARD, PHD, ABPP, MARIANNE CELANO, PHD, ABPP, AND

MARIETTA COLLINS, PHD

ILLUSTRATED BY KEITH HENRY BROWN

MAGINATION PRESS • WASHINGTON, DC • AMERICAN PSYCHOLOGICAL ASSOCIATION

To artists and activists of all ages: Together we can claim peace and create community—AH, MC, & MC

I dedicate this book to all of the little brown boys and girls who love to draw. Keep it up! Don't get discouraged. You'll get there—KHB

Books for Kids from the
American Psychological Association.

Copyright © 2021 by Magination Press, an imprint of the American Psychological Association. Illustrations copyright © 2021 by Keith Henry Brown. All rights reserved. Except as permitted under the United States Copyright Act of 1976, no part of this publication may be reproduced or distributed in any form or by any means, or stored in a database or retrieval system, without the prior written permission of the publisher.

Magination Press is a registered trademark of the American Psychological Association. Order books at maginationpress.org, or call 1-800-374-2721.

Book design by Rachel Ross
Printed by Phoenix Color, Hagerstown, MD

Library of Congress Cataloging-in-Publication Data
Names: Hazzard, Ann, author. | Celano, Marianne, author. | Collins, Marietta, author. | Brown, Keith Henry, illustrator.
Title: Something happened in our park : standing together after gun violence / by Ann Hazzard, PhD, ABPP, Marianne Celano, PhD, ABPP, and Marietta Collins, PhD ; illustrated by Keith Henry Brown.
Description: Washington, D.C. : Magination Press, [2021] | Miles wants to move away after his cousin Keisha is accidentally shot in their neighborhood park, but Keisha and Miles' father work with others to make their community a safer place.
Identifiers: LCCN 2020030382 (print) | LCCN 2020030383 (ebook) | ISBN 9781433835216 (hardcover) | ISBN 9781433835223 (ebook)
Subjects: CYAC: Violence—Fiction. | Anxiety—Fiction. | Parks—Fiction. | Community life—Fiction. | Family life—Fiction.
Classification: LCC PZ7.1.H3973 Som 2021 (print) | LCC PZ7.1.H3973 (ebook) | DDC [E]—dc23
LC record available at https://lccn.loc.gov/2020030382
LC ebook record available at https://lccn.loc.gov/2020030383

Manufactured in the United States of America
10 9 8 7 6 5 4 3 2 1

"Something bad happened in our park last night," said Miles' dad. "Keisha was shot in the leg, but she's okay. She'll be home from the hospital tomorrow."

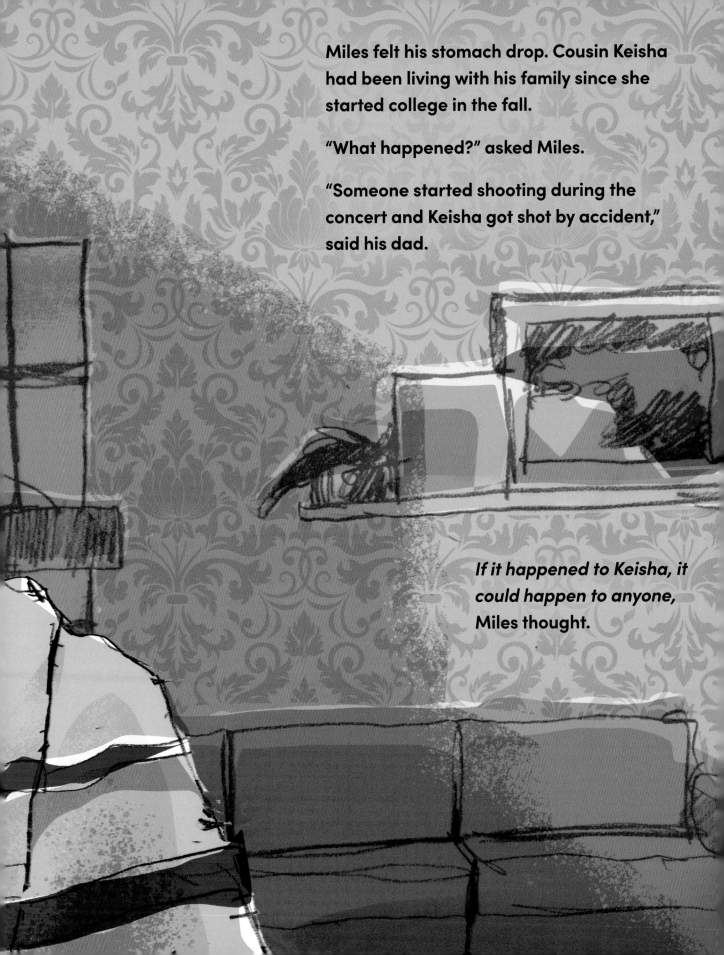

Miles felt his stomach drop. Cousin Keisha had been living with his family since she started college in the fall.

"What happened?" asked Miles.

"Someone started shooting during the concert and Keisha got shot by accident," said his dad.

If it happened to Keisha, it could happen to anyone, Miles thought.

The next week at school, Miles got in trouble twice for daydreaming. Instead of doing his work, he drew picture after picture. His teacher sent the scariest picture home to his parents with a note.

"Oh no!" said his mother. "Is this our neighborhood? It looks frightening!"

"It is," said Miles. "I wish there were no guns here. I want to move somewhere else!"

"There is less money and more violence here since the factory closed. But we can't afford to move."

"This is where your dad and I grew up.
There's a lot that we love about this place.

Like Grandma B's red velvet cake and the
8th Avenue church choir!"

His dad said,
"The most important
thing is that the
people here care
for each other."

Two weeks later, Keisha was watching Miles and his little brother Marcus.

They had just finished dinner when they heard three loud pops.

Miles felt his stomach drop again. "Are those gunshots?"

Keisha seemed frozen at first. Then, she took charge. "I'm not sure, but we're safe here. Let's all take a deep breath. We can't control what's happening out there. But, we can stay calm and keep living our lives."

"But how?" asked Miles.

"Let's do something you enjoy," said Keisha.
"How about drawing a picture together?"

When his mom got home, she
found a surprise on the fridge.

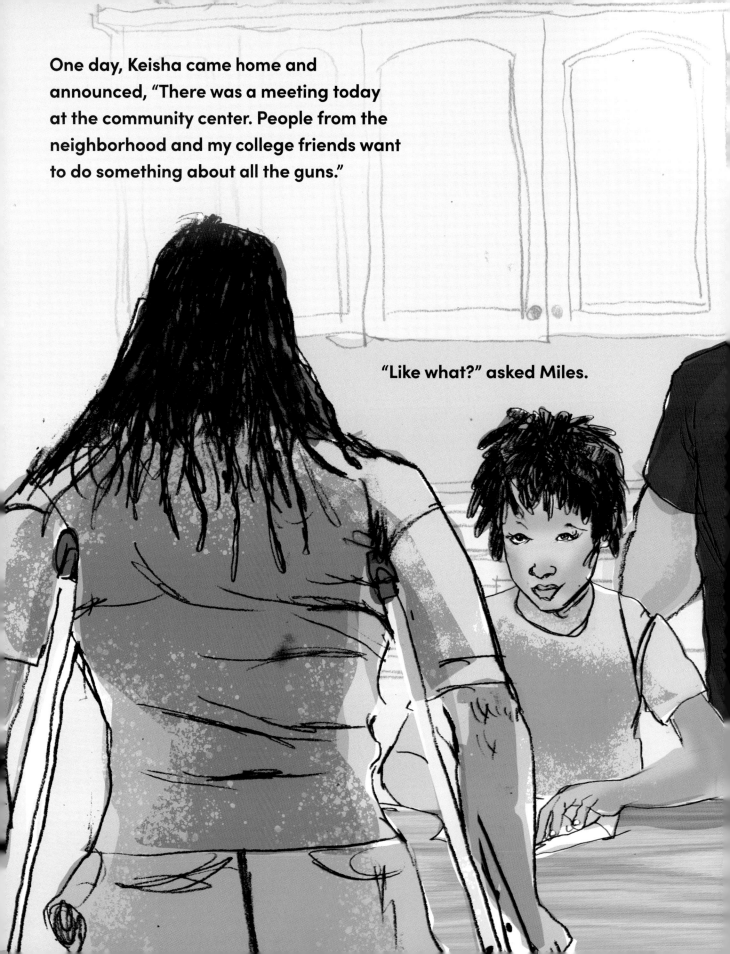

One day, Keisha came home and announced, "There was a meeting today at the community center. People from the neighborhood and my college friends want to do something about all the guns."

"Like what?" asked Miles.

"We're planning to meet with the mayor to ask for money for a community safety program."

"I'll go with you to the next meeting!" said Miles' dad.

When Keisha got back from winter break, Miles' dad told her the good news. The mayor had agreed to fund the "Peace in the Streets" project.

"Finally, this neighborhood is getting its fair share! You really helped get the ball rolling," he said.

Keisha was back to her cheerful self. She even went out at night with her friends.

For Miles, it was different. Most days he felt okay, but sometimes scary scenes popped into his mind. And he always stayed away from the windows at night.

Soon, it was time for the Spring Festival at the park. Miles' friend David texted to ask Miles and Marcus to go to the festival with his family.

"I don't think we can," said Miles.

"Why did you say that?" asked his mom. "Your father and I have to work. You could go have fun."

Miles whispered,
"What if there is
another shooting?"

"I know you're worried, and I am too. But we can't keep avoiding the park. If we don't claim it, who will? There will be lots of neighbors there who care about you and want to make the park safe. I bet the 'Peace in the Streets' program will also be getting started!"

Miles sat down and drew a picture of how he wanted the park to be. It was peaceful and beautiful.

He decided that he would go to the festival after all.

At the
festival...

Miles saw a booth where people were signing up for summer activities.

"Keisha and Dad helped the city to start that program!" he told David. Miles decided to sign up for art camp. He had a great idea for how to make the park more beautiful.

A year after the shooting,
the mayor was speaking
in the park.

Miles and Keisha saw David and some other kids running around the track. "Is that Officer Jones out there?" asked Miles.

"Yeah," said Keisha. "Cops are coaching the track team!"

Mayor Wilson started the ceremony by saying, "Violence ends when dreams begin." She announced the opening of a bread company in the neighborhood, with 100 new jobs.

Keisha talked about everybody working together and led a "People Power" cheer.

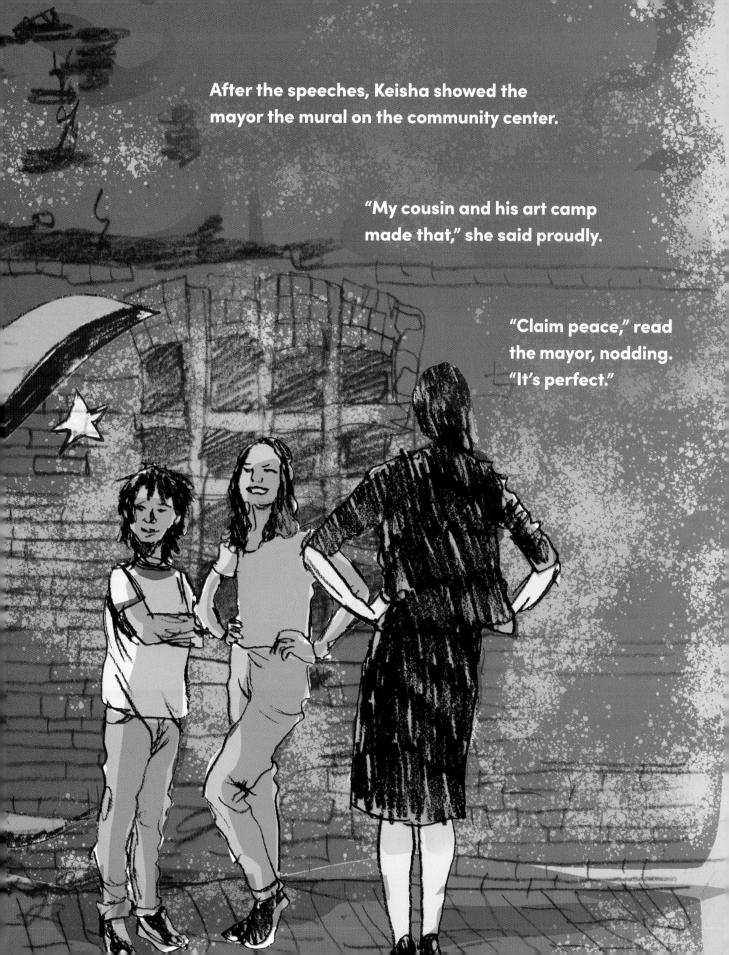

After the speeches, Keisha showed the
mayor the mural on the community center.

"My cousin and his art camp
made that," she said proudly.

"Claim peace," read
the mayor, nodding.
"It's perfect."

Miles smiled.

READER'S NOTE

Something Happened in Our Park features child and teen characters who cope with a shooting in their neighborhood. Sadly, many children in the United States have been exposed to gun violence. Some have experienced or witnessed shootings in their communities, while others have heard media stories or accounts from older children or adults.

We hope that the story will facilitate constructive discussions about community safety in your family or classroom. These discussions can help children understand gun violence in a developmentally appropriate manner, distinguish between real and perceived threats to safety, and manage anxiety about gun violence in their own lives and communities. In addition, adults can introduce children to the root causes of community gun violence, such as structural racism and income disparities.

Talking about gun violence is challenging. However, avoiding the topic is likely to leave many children struggling with anxiety on their own. Discussing the story can cultivate hope and empower children to be part of violence prevention efforts in their communities.

INCIDENCE AND IMPACT OF GUN VIOLENCE

Every year over 15,000 U.S. children and teens (ages 0–19) are killed or injured by shootings, an average of 43 per day. An estimated three million children witness a shooting each year. This is not a problem we can ignore.

The majority of firearm assaults on children and teens occur in urban areas. Furthermore, Black and Latino children are particularly likely to be impacted by gun violence. For example, Black boys are 10 times more likely to be hospitalized for a firearm injury than White boys.

Why are Black and Latino youth so disproportionately impacted? Gun violence tends to be concentrated in specific "hot spots" in some urban neighborhoods. These neighborhoods have been created by local and national policy decisions over many years which promoted residential segregation and economic divestment (e.g. underfunded school systems, limited job opportunities). Hopeless and frustrated individuals in these neighborhoods may engage in violent crime, contributing to a vicious cycle of neighborhood disadvantage.

Also, the relationship between Black communities and the police has been complicated by history. In the past, police aggressively enforced Jim Crow laws. Currently, racial profiling by police and disproportionate use of force against Black individuals is well documented. Furthermore, police bias is one component of a racist criminal justice system that has resulted in mass incarceration of Black men. For all of these reasons, many Black individuals don't trust the police to consistently promote community safety. Hopefully, the relationship between the police and communities of color may improve with recent efforts to reduce bias, increase accountability, and broadly "re-imagine" policing.

Exposure to community violence puts children at increased risk for a variety of negative psychological outcomes. These children spend less time outside and are more likely to suffer from depression, anxiety, and post-traumatic stress disorder. Additionally, emotional concerns and concentration problems may contribute to poorer academic performance. However, it is important to note that the majority of ethnic minority children raised in poverty and exposed to adversities have positive outcomes, due to their own resilience and family and community support.

Mass shootings, some of which have occurred in school settings, have received more media attention than community-based gun violence. As public concern about mass shootings has increased, many children have participated in armed intruder drills in their schools. Unfortunately, there is little evidence that drills prevent school shootings or injuries, and they potentially increase children's anxiety.

We chose to focus on community gun violence in *Something Happened in Our Park*, as this type of violence is more common than mass shootings and is an overlooked and under-resourced problem. The story may be particularly relevant to families experiencing community violence. However, children living in relatively safer communities can also benefit from this story. In today's uncertain times, all children are likely to empathize with Miles' fears. Regardless of their backgrounds, children will be inspired by how Miles and other community members work together to "claim peace" in their neighborhood.

HELPING CHILDREN COPE WITH ANXIETY

We all want our children to feel safe. Yet, we also want to prepare them for dangers that they may face. At times, this preparation might increase their anxiety, although appropriate education also increases children's actual safety. These are competing priorities, and finding the right balance is challenging.

For communities experiencing gun violence, two types of strategies are helpful. Individual and family-level strategies are often targeted towards reducing risk for particular children and increasing their ability to cope with anxiety. Community-based strategies typically aim to reduce actual gun violence, often while enhancing community well-being more broadly. To be successful, these efforts must be spearheaded by adults in the community and partners with political and economic power, such as government officials and business leaders.

Individual and Family Strategies to Increase Safety and Reduce Anxiety

Shootings occur much more often in the United States than in comparable income countries. Like Miles, children who become aware of shootings may become fearful and want to avoid certain activities or places. Other symptoms of anxiety are sleep and appetite changes, physical complaints, concentration problems, clinginess, irritability, or behavior problems.

Parents have an important role in helping children cope with anxiety. Children sense when caretakers are stressed, so it is important for parents to develop strategies to manage their own feelings. For stress management tips for adults, see the "For More Information" section at the end of this Note.

Children also rely on parents to help them understand and manage their feelings. These approaches may be helpful:

- Limit your children's exposure to graphic violent imagery in the news or in other media such as video games.
- Ask your children questions to find out what information they have and how they are feeling. For example, after reading the story, you could say, "Miles was worried after the park shooting. Have you ever felt like that?" If you are discussing a violent incident in your community or in the news, you could start with, "What have you heard about (the event)?"
- Discuss your children's reactions and concerns. Validate their feelings.
- Help your children manage their reactions, using some of the strategies below. These three approaches are designed to help children cope with feelings, thoughts, and behaviors.

Expressing Feelings: You can help your children manage stress by coaching them to "turn down the volume" on emotions that feel overwhelming. For example, Miles' cousin helps him use deep breathing and drawing to calm himself down. Other emotion regulation techniques include 1) humming or singing, 2) snuggling with a pet or favorite cuddly object, and 3) visualizing a safe place, a positive memory, or a situation in which your child mastered something scary. Any activity which helps your child feel empowered (e.g. music, sports, prayer) can help to balance feelings of vulnerability.

Encouraging Positive Thinking: Positive thinking does *not* mean sugar-coating problems or providing blanket reassurances. It *does* mean trying to help your child think realistically about risk. Yes, the risk of our children being victims of gun violence is much higher than it should be. At the same time, a minority of children are victims of gun violence, even in higher-crime neighborhoods. Children are much more likely to die in a car accident than a mass shooting. In the "Adult-Child Dialogues" section below, we give some examples of how you might help your child evaluate risk realistically.

If you are a parent with concerns about the safety of your neighborhood, you might coach your children to develop future-oriented goals which motivate positive behaviors. For example, you could emphasize the importance of doing well in school in order to get a good job that will provide broader choices of where to live. If you are the parent of a Black child, you may also encourage racial pride. You could say, "Our ancestors were strong enough to survive slavery and a lot of unfair treatment after that. We will survive this shooting. Let's think of some ways that we are strong."

Taking Action: As a parent, you want your children to benefit from school and other daily activities. In the story, Miles' mother tells him, "We can't keep avoiding the park. If we don't claim it, who will?" She is helping him to face his fears, live his life, and be part of a neighborhood revitalization effort.

You might decide to increase home security features and tell your children about what you are doing to make your home safe. You could counsel children about actions that they can take to increase personal safety. Many parents encourage children to avoid specific dangerous areas and situations and affiliate with peers engaging in prosocial behaviors.

The topic of personal safety leads us to the issue of parental gun ownership. Some parents believe that having a gun in the home increases risk. Other parents feel that owning a gun enables them to better protect themselves and their families. If you are a parent who does own a gun, it is very important to follow expert guidelines for safe storage (see the "For More Information" section). When guns are not stored safely, there is greater risk that young children may get injured accidentally and that teens may use the gun to threaten or hurt themselves or others. Safe storage can help to prevent these tragedies.

Community Strategies to Reduce Gun Violence

In this story, adults from Miles' family and neighborhood work with college students and government officials in a multi-faceted effort to make their community safer. A centerpiece of their initiative is a new business with jobs for community members, since lack of economic opportunity contributes significantly to gun violence. Secondly, the story's "Peace in the Streets" program represents a "focused deterrence" program, similar to those successfully implemented in multiple U.S. cities. These interdisciplinary programs identify the relatively small number of individuals repeatedly involved in shootings and incentivize them to avoid violence and re-engage constructively with the community. Youth

development and mentoring programs represent a third approach and have demonstrated effectiveness in promoting prosocial behaviors, enhancing coping skills, and reducing violence. In Miles' neighborhood, a mentoring program is established by local police officers, one aspect of a more collaborative community policing approach. Drug courts and treatment options have also been found to reduce recidivism, in contrast with incarceration. A final community-level strategy is advocacy for legislative changes likely to reduce gun violence. Diverse organizations advocate universal background checks for gun purchasers, laws to keep guns away from domestic abusers and suicidal individuals, laws to reduce gun trafficking, and laws to mandate secure gun storage.

Note: For readers wanting more information about gun violence and prevention strategies, references can be found in the online resources for this book. See the "For More Information" section.

ADULT-CHILD DIALOGUES

This section includes sample responses to questions from children, as well as some conversation-starting tips for parents or educators. Some of the adult-initiated conversations will be more appropriate for children who identify with Miles and his community, whereas others may be best suited for children who may initially see Miles and his neighborhood as very "different" from them. Reading the story can help increase their empathy for his experiences and recognize similarities between families facing diverse life circumstances.

In general, it is best to allow children to lead the discussion. When children ask questions, you can elicit their ideas first by asking "What do you think?" If you are answering a question, be honest and succinct and avoid lectures. It's okay to say, "I don't know, let me think about it," if you need some time to formulate a response.

Note: Adult responses are in black text whereas child responses are in purple text.

Questions From Children

- **Why did the person in the park have a gun?** I'm not sure and we don't always know why people have guns in real life. Many people believe that it is safer not to have guns at home. Other adults buy guns to protect themselves and their families, in case someone tries to harm them. But because guns can really hurt you, it is important for adults who own guns to put them in a safe and secret place and lock them up. Sometimes children or teenagers find guns that adults did not store safely. If you see or find a gun that is not locked up, you should never pick it up. If it is loaded, it could go off and hurt someone. You should find an adult and tell them about the gun.

- **Can anyone get a gun?** No, only adults can legally buy a gun. If you are 21 years old and correctly answer questions on a form, then you can buy a gun. However, sometimes people buy or borrow guns from others without filling out forms. Owning a gun is a big responsibility because guns can be used to hurt people. For this reason, many other countries limit or regulate gun ownership more strongly than the United States does.

- **Is our neighborhood safe?** People in our neighborhood watch out for each other by keeping an eye out for anything dangerous (like cars going too fast, or break-ins) and talking with one another about what they see or hear. We try our best so that you can enjoy being a kid and not have to worry about being safe. The police also help to make our neighborhood safe, especially when they work with us to establish trust. No neigborhood is 100 percent safe, but listening to us and obeying our family rules will help keep you safe. (An additional response for a neighborhood with safety concerns might be "There have been some shootings in our neighborhood. But, even so, most people do not ever get shot. Think about all of the people on our street who have *not* gotten shot.")

- **Does this mean I shouldn't go to the park? Are parks safe?** Most parks are safe; the adults in our neigborhood work together to make sure that everyone can safely enjoy parks. We don't want fears about safety to keep you from enjoying parks with your friends and family.

- **How do I stay safe when people around me may have guns?** It is scary to think that someone around you might have a gun. That thought would make most people worried for their safety. But most people do not carry guns around with them. We try to choose places that are safe for you to go, so that you won't have to worry about guns. It is our job to love and protect you.

- **What can we do to keep our neighborhood safe? Our house safe?** Let's think of all the people who are helping to keep us safe: parents, grandparents, teachers, shopkeepers, librarians, police, fire fighters, doctors...can you think of anyone else? We keep our house safe by having smoke alarms, locks on doors, windows that keep out the rain, and our dog. We keep each other safe by keeping track of where everybody is and by talking to one another if one of us feels unsafe or uncomfortable in a new place.

- **Most of the people in this story are Black. Are all Black neighborhoods dangerous?** Most of the people in Miles' neighborhood are Black. But not all Black neighborhoods are dangerous. When neighborhoods are dangerous it is usually because there are fewer jobs and fewer people working together to make it safe. When people have money to feed their families, there is less crime. That's true for all neighborhoods, whether mostly Black, White, or other people of color live there. Also, when people look out for one another and trust one another, the neighborhood is safer.

- **Why are there so many shootings in Miles' neighborhood?** One reason might be that it is easy for people in our country to buy guns. Maybe people don't feel safe, so they buy guns, but some don't store and use them safely. Maybe there are not enough jobs for everyone, or the jobs don't pay enough for the families to survive. This situation makes it difficult for people to make good decisions for themselves and their families. Some people might even do dangerous things (like gambling, stealing, or selling drugs) to get money, and they may use guns to settle disputes. There are usually very few people using guns this way in most neighborhoods. But they can make life scary for the people who are obeying the law and not hurting others.

- **Why didn't Miles' family move to a different place?** Miles' dad said they didn't have enough money to move. Also, they wanted to stay near their church, school, friends, and family in their community. And, what would happen if all the families moved away? Miles' dad wanted to work to make his community safer instead of giving up and moving to a new neighborhood.

- **Why didn't Keisha go back to staying with her parents?** Keisha was living with her cousin Miles and his parents so that she could attend college nearby. Her parents lived further away, and if she lived with them it would be harder for her to get to her college classes. Keisha is part of Miles' family. Some families are small, including just parents and one or two kids; others are large, including cousins, aunts, uncles, and grandparents.

- **Why didn't Miles' mother or father stay home to protect him?** Miles' parents sometimes were away from home at their jobs. They needed to work to make money to pay for things that the family needed. They trusted Keisha to take care of Miles and Marcus when they were working. Plus, they took steps to keep the family safe, like putting locks on doors and staying in touch by phone.

- **Why did Miles' mother tell him to go to the park even though he was scared?** She believed the park was safe at that time. She didn't want to live in fear, and she didn't want her son to live in fear either. Miles' mother knew that shootings make people sad and scared. It's okay to have those feelings about a shooting, but we should also live our lives as fully as we can. Miles' mother is also taking steps to protect her children, and he may not know about all those steps.

Conversations Initiated by Adults

The first set of questions could be posed by caretakers or teachers to help children better understand story themes of 1) coping with anxiety and 2) community empowerment. The second section provides ideas for facilitating discussions of underlying social issues that contribute to community gun violence.

Note: The purple text indicates concepts that adults can elicit from children during these discussions.

Discussing Story Themes

- What did Miles' parents (or Keisha) do to make him feel safer? **They listened to him and reassured him that there are lots of people who care about him and want to keep him safe. They didn't make him feel bad or silly for being afraid. They showed him the importance of neighbors and government officials working together to make their neighborhood safe.**

- What did Miles do to make himself feel safer? **He told the adults in his life about how he was feeling. Keisha showed him how to use art to express how he was feeling, to calm himself,**

and to visualize a positive future. He learned to not let his fears control him or keep him from enjoying life.

- We read some negative and positive things about Miles' neighborhood when Keisha got shot. What were the problems? **Miles drew it as a scary place because of the shooting. His father talked about a factory closing.** What were the good things about the neighborhood? **His parents talked about the things they love about the neighborhood. It's where they grew up and a place where their family, friends, and church are located.** What do the pictures show? [Point to illustrations that show both of these features of the neighborhood].

- What was Miles' community like a year later (at the ceremony)? **The park has a new mural. Many people are involved in positive activities (the "Peace in the Streets" festival, police coaching the neighborhood track team). A new company has opened with more jobs for the community.** What do the pictures show? [Point to illustrations that show these aspects of the neighborhood].

- Miles' mural said, "Claim peace." What did people in the neighborhood do to make their community safer and more peaceful? **Miles' father, Keisha, and her college friends began going to meetings with city officials and pushing for positive changes. The mayor and city officials responded by giving money for a community safety program and improving the park. They also helped a new company to open in the neighborhood. These changes resulted in neighbors feeling safer, taking pride in the community, and participating in family activities. They reclaimed the neighborhood for the people who loved it and this made it safer.**

- The mayor said, "Violence ends when dreams begin." What do you think she meant? **If people can follow their dreams, then they won't be violent. Crime and gun violence increase when people don't think they can have a good future.**

- What would you like to paint on a mural to inspire a positive change in your community?

- What does this book make you think about in your life?

Exploring Social Issues

Poverty, racist policies, and the prevalence of guns in the United States have all contributed to elevated levels of gun violence. This story can be used as a springboard for discussions of these root causes of violence. It is important to help children understand contextual factors so that they do not adopt and promote racist explanations for gun violence. For example, the myth that Black individuals are more violent has been consistently utilized to justify racist policies. This inaccurate and harmful stereotype can lead to blaming the victim and deter policy reforms aimed at producing equitable opportunities. The section below contains some key concepts that an adult might introduce and some questions which can facilitate further reflection.

- **Residential segregation:** Miles and most of his neighbors appear to be Black. Let's talk about why there are many neighborhoods that are segregated (that means mostly people of one race live there). There was a time when White people didn't want Black people to live near them, so they let them buy houses only in certain parts of the city. Sometimes these parts of the city didn't have a lot of trees, and the houses were small. The Black people who lived there didn't make enough money to move to a better area, or they wanted to stay there to be with their friends and family. Another reason may be that White people used to live in Miles' community, but moved away when more Black families moved in because they didn't want to live in the same community as Black people or have their children go to the same schools. What do you think it's called when people exclude or move away from others because of their skin color or race? **Racism, discrimination.** Do you think housing segregation is fair? **No, everyone should be able to live where they want. If people of different races lived in the same neighborhood, they could probably get to know and respect each other.**

- **Income and wealth disparities:** Many things have happened in the United States that made it harder for Black people to make enough money to house, clothe, and feed their families. When Black people were forced to be slaves, how did this affect their ability to take care of their families? **They had to depend on White owners for everything and were not paid any money for their work.** When White owners sold the crops farmed by enslaved Black Americans, who got to keep the money? **The White owners got to keep all the money.** Yes, slavery

was set up so that White Americans got richer and Black Americans got nothing. White Americans got a giant, unfair head start on making money. Even today, White Americans own most of the businesses in the United States and many businesses are not fair about hiring and promoting Black Americans.

- **Gun violence:** The United States has more gun violence than many countries. Why do you think that might be? **Many countries have strict laws against citizens buying or owning certain types of guns. The United States does not, so it is pretty easy to buy a gun and there are more guns around.**

- **Solutions:** What can be done to help neighborhoods that are poor or have problems with shootings? **More jobs; programs to help kids achieve their dreams; neighbors working together; good relationships between police and neighbors; laws that make it harder for criminals to get guns; keeping guns locked up safely.**

*Note: Our capitalization of Black acknowledges a shared culture which has been consciously claimed and celebrated. Our capitalization of White is an acknowledgment that Whiteness confers social benefits, but not an endorsement of White claims of virtue or superiority. Our capitalization of White represents an attempt to make Whiteness visible, in service of antiracism.

FOR MORE INFORMATION

Further free information is available on the web at apa.org/pubs/magination/something-happened-in-our-park. There you will find:

1) Two booklists for children which include books related to

   a. Poverty, Resilience, and Community Empowerment

   b. Overcoming Anxiety

2) Resources for adults, including

   a. Stress Management Strategies for Parents

   b. Gun Safety Recommendations

   c. Additional Resources for Educators

   d. References for this Reader's Note, including information about gun violence and prevention approaches

ABOUT THE ILLUSTRATIONS

I decided pretty early on upon reading the manuscript that I wanted to give the art a looser, more spontaneous feel. I wanted the story to have a timeless quality, and for the reader to feel as if the events are actually happening. I imagined sketching everything out as if I were in the environment with the characters themselves—live, somewhat as a court reporting artist would. The feeling I hoped for is that things are moving and that nothing is static. I then scanned the drawings on separate pieces of paper, and then layered them in together with Photoshop, also using bits of collage elements.

The loose lines serve to take away the feeling of solidity so that we feel a certain sense of anxiousness, as if there is movement in the story even when people are standing still.—**KHB**

ANN HAZZARD, PHD, ABPP, MARIANNA CELANO, PHD, ABPP, and **MARIETTA COLLINS, PHD,** worked together for over two decades as Emory University School of Medicine faculty members, serving children and families in Atlanta. All three psychologists have been involved in community advocacy efforts focused on children's behavioral health and social justice. Dr. Celano and Dr. Hazzard have developed and utilized therapeutic stories in individual and group therapy with children and teens. Dr. Collins is a faculty member at Morehouse School of Medicine, providing psychological services to underserved adults, youth, and families.

KEITH HENRY BROWN is an artist and illustrator who has drawn comics for Marvel as well as created watercolor paintings for greeting cards, newspapers, magazines, books, and album covers. He lives in Brooklyn, NY. Visit keithhbrown.com and @iamtheleopard on Instagram.

MAGINATION PRESS is the children's book imprint of the American Psychological Association. APA works to advance psychology as a science and profession and as a means of promoting health and human welfare. Magination Press books reach young readers and their parents and caregivers to make navigating life's challenges a little easier. It's the combined power of psychology and literature that makes a Magination Press book special. Visit maginationpress.org and @MaginationPress on Facebook, Twitter, Instagram, and Pinterest.